Dear Parents:

Congratulations! Your child is taking the first steps on an exciting journey. The destination? Independent reading!

STEP INTO READING® will help your child get there. The program offers five steps to reading success. Each step includes fun stories and colorful art or photographs. In addition to original fiction and books with favorite characters, there are Step into Reading Non-Fiction Readers, Phonics Readers and Boxed Sets, Sticker Readers, and Comic Readers—a complete literacy program with something to interest every child.

Learning to Read, Step by Step!

Ready to Read   Preschool–Kindergarten
• big type and easy words • rhyme and rhythm • picture clues
For children who know the alphabet and are eager to begin reading.

Reading with Help   Preschool–Grade 1
• basic vocabulary • short sentences • simple stories
For children who recognize familiar words and sound out new words with help.

Reading on Your Own   Grades 1–3
• engaging characters • easy-to-follow plots • popular topics
For children who are ready to read on their own.

Reading Paragraphs   Grades 2–3
• challenging vocabulary • short paragraphs • exciting stories
For newly independent readers who read simple sentences with confidence.

Ready for Chapters   Grades 2–4
• chapters • longer paragraphs • full-color art
For children who want to take the plunge into chapter books but still like colorful pictures.

STEP INTO READING® is designed to give every child a successful reading experience. The grade levels are only guides; children will progress through the steps at their own speed, developing confidence in their reading.

Remember, a lifetime love of reading starts with a single step!

Copyright © 2014 Disney Enterprises, Inc. All rights reserved. Published
in the United States by Random House Children's Books, a division of
Random House LLC, 1745 Broadway, New York, NY 10019, and in Canada
by Random House of Canada Limited, Toronto, Penguin Random House
Companies, in conjunction with Disney Enterprises, Inc.

Step into Reading, Random House, and the Random House colophon
are registered trademarks of Random House LLC.

Visit us on the Web!
StepIntoReading.com
randomhousekids.com

Educators and librarians, for a variety of teaching tools,
visit us at RHTeachersLibrarians.com

ISBN 978-0-7364-3189-7 (trade) — ISBN 978-0-7364-8160-1 (lib. bdg.)
ISBN 978-0-7364-3190-3 (ebook)

Printed in the United States of America   10 9 8 7 6 5 4 3 2 1

STEP 3
STEP
READING ON YOUR OWN

STEP INTO READING®

Disney

BIG HERO 6

FIGHT
TO THE
FINISH!

By Bill Scollon

Illustrated by the Disney Storybook Art Team

Random House 🏠 New York

Hiro is a high school graduate.

He is only fourteen.

He is a robotics genius!

Hiro's friends are also smart.

Honey Lemon takes pictures
when she mixes chemicals.
Wasabi loves cleaning
and studying physics.
Go Go Tomago knows about
engineering.
Fred is a fan of
monsters and
comic books.

Hiro is working hard on
tiny robots called microbots.
He hopes to win a scholarship
at the Tech Showcase.
He wants to attend
a college robotics program.
Professor Callaghan teaches it.

Hiro presents his invention.

He wears a transmitter on his head

to control the bots with his mind.

The bots can form anything

Hiro imagines!

Hiro's invention is a hit!

Billionaire Alistair Krei looks at

the amazing microbots.

Krei offers to buy them,

but Hiro does not want to sell.

After the showcase,

the building catches fire!

Hiro's microbots are still inside.

He won't be able to save them!

Back home, Hiro stubs his toe.

"Ow!"

Suddenly, he hears a noise.

It is a robot

filling with air!

"Hello. I am Baymax," he says.

"I am your nurse bot."

Baymax and Hiro become friends.

Then Hiro sees a microbot.

The microbot leads them

to an old warehouse.

The door is locked.

Baymax helps Hiro

sneak through a window.

Hiro finds thousands of microbots.

He thought all his bots

had been destroyed.

But somebody stole his invention

and made more!

Suddenly, a huge swarm of microbots

chases Hiro and Baymax.

"Run!" yells Hiro.

Who is controlling the bots?

Hiro sees a man
wearing a mask!
He is controlling the microbots!
The sharp microbots hit Baymax
and poke holes in his vinyl skin.

Hiro and Baymax escape.

Baymax uses tape

to fix the holes.

Hiro wants to find out
who the masked man is.
He teaches Baymax karate moves
and makes him a suit of armor.

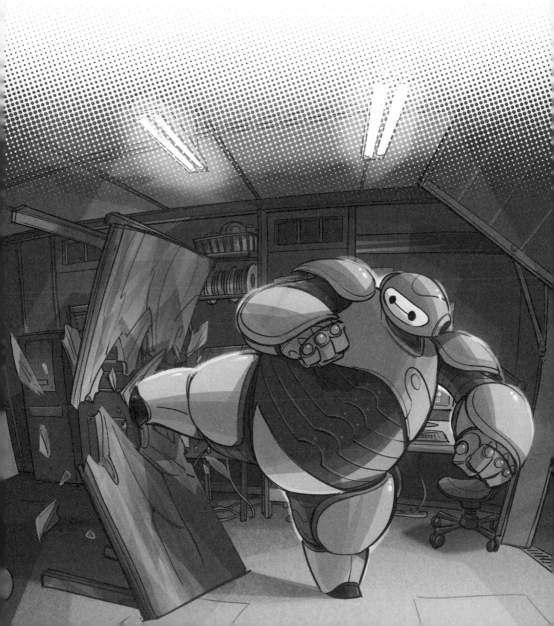

Baymax kicks in the door
at the warehouse.
The building is empty.
Where are all the microbots
and the masked man?

A car pulls up.

Hiro's friends have come!

"What are you doing?"

asks Wasabi.

Hiro doesn't want his friends
to get hurt.
"You guys need to go!" he says.

The man in the mask appears.
He uses a huge group of microbots
to throw a heavy crate at Hiro
and his friends.

"We're under attack by a super villain!"
yells Fred.

Baymax protects Fred and the others
as they run to the car.

The friends try to get away.

They race through the streets.

The masked man is catching up.

The car crashes into the bay!

It begins to fill with water.

The masked man watches them sink.

He does not see

Baymax throw off his armor

and float everyone to the surface.

They go to Fred's house.

It is a mansion!

Everyone agrees to help Hiro

catch the man in the mask.

But Hiro knows
that Baymax
needs more upgrades.
They all do!

Hiro makes armor for everyone.

Go Go gets wheels

and throwing discs.

"Got to say, I like it!" she says.

Hiro gives Honey
a purse full of chemicals.
She can use them to make
any kind of high-tech mixture.
"I love it! I love it!" she shouts.

Wasabi's suit has laser hands
that can cut through anything!
"Whoa!" he says.

Fred wears a monster costume
that breathes fire.

It can also super-jump!

"This is the best day of my life,"
he tells the group.

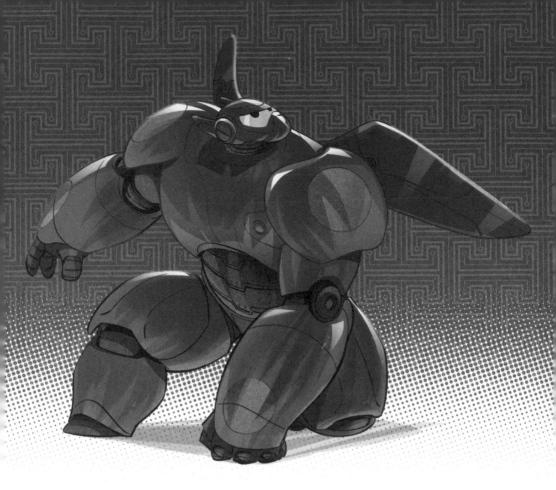

Hiro has saved the best for Baymax.

Baymax gets new armor,

rocket fists, a super sensor,

and wings.

"I fail to see how flying

makes me a better nurse bot,"

he tells Hiro.

"Because flying is awesome!" Hiro says, putting on his own battle suit.

Hiro jumps onto Baymax's back.

Flying is not as easy as it looks.

"Up, up! Look out!" Hiro shouts.

"Full thrust! Level out!"

Soon Hiro and Baymax

are zooming across the sky.

Baymax uses his new super sensor
to scan the city.
He finds the man in the mask.
The villain is on Akuma Island.

Hiro and his team confront him

in an old laboratory.

The microbots attack the heroes.

"Go for the mask," Hiro says.

"That's how he controls the bots."

Wasabi cuts through the bots
with his laser hands.
But the masked man
knocks him into a wall.

Go Go attacks next!

Then Honey tries!

He defeats the heroes

one by one.

Even Fred's fire-breathing suit
is no match for the microbots.
Hiro jumps at the bad guy
and grabs for his mask.

The mask falls off.

It's Professor Callaghan!

Hiro moves in to capture him,

but the professor escapes.

Callaghan hates Alistair Krei.

Krei once experimented

with a portal machine.

But the portal was not safe.

It broke with the pilot inside.

The pilot's name was Abigail.

She was the professor's daughter!

Callaghan traps Krei.

The microbots make a new portal.

The professor wants revenge!

He tries to throw Krei into the portal.

But the heroes stop him

by working as a team.

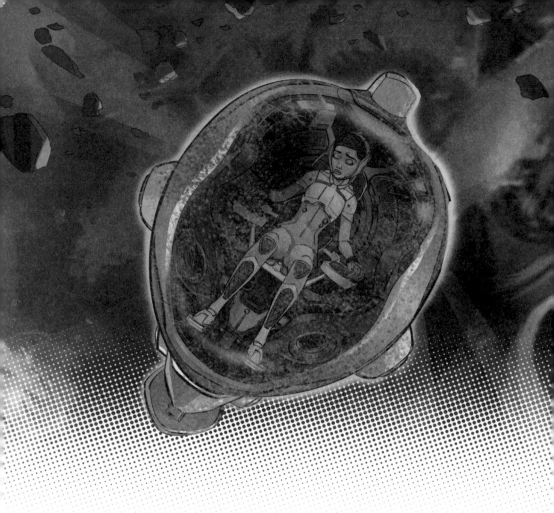

Baymax scans the portal
and finds signs of life.
It's Abigail!
He and Hiro rush in to save her,
but the portal is closing.
They have to get out fast!

Baymax is damaged in the portal.

He can't fly.

His rocket fist

can save Hiro and Abigail.

But Baymax has to stay behind.

Hiro sadly says goodbye

to his friend.

Hiro and his friends

miss Baymax.

Then Hiro finds something

inside the rocket fist.

It's the computer chip

that made Baymax who he was!

Hiro uses the chip

to make a new Baymax.

"Hello," says the new robot.

"I am Baymax, your nurse bot."

Hiro and his friends
are happy that Baymax is back.
Together, they are Big Hero 6!